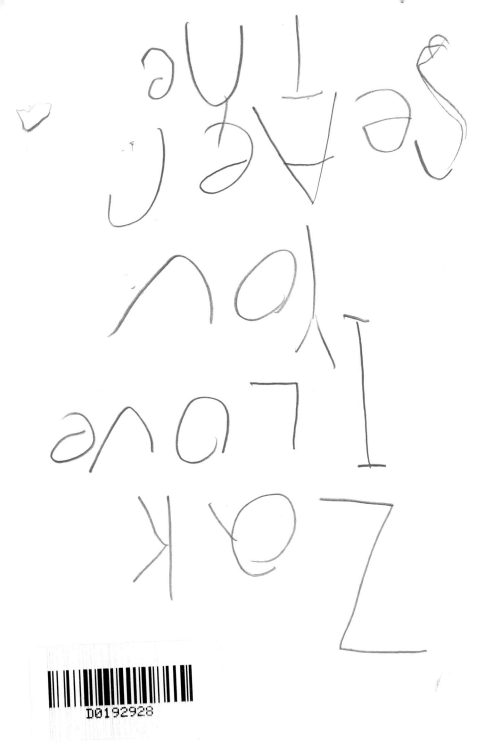

seAterTue
you
I Love
Zak

GHOULFRIENDS

THE GHOUL-IT-YOURSELF BOOK

CREEPY COOL

Little, Brown and Company

Hachette Book Group
237 Park Avenue, New York, NY 10017
Visit our website at lb-kids.com

Little, Brown and Company is a division of
Hachette Book Group, Inc.
The Little, Brown name and logo
are trademarks of Hachette Book Group, Inc.

The publisher is not responsible for websites (or their content) that are not owned by the publisher.

First Edition: September 2014

Library of Congress Control Number: 2014934949

ISBN 978-0-316-28222-2

10 9 8 7 6 5 4 3 2 1

RRD-C

Printed in the United States of America

GHOULFRIENDS

THE GHOUL-IT-YOURSELF BOOK

GITTY DANESHVARI

WITH

POLLYGEIST DANESCARY

LITTLE, BROWN AND COMPANY

NEW YORK • BOSTON

Be yourself
BE UNIQUE
BE A
MONSTER

contents

Ghoulfriends Forever
at Monster High!

as three of the newest members of Monster High's student disembody, Rochelle Goyle, Robecca Steam, and Venus McFlytrap are in for a wild ride—and you're going to join them! On top of Catacombing, Ghoulish Literature, and all their other classes, the ghouls find themselves joining in on school clubs and activities, bonding with their new beasties, and even solving a gripping mystery.

It's time for you and your ghoulfriends to dive into Venus's compost pile, take a turn in the limelight at the Hex Factor Talon Show, and go for the gold on Crack and Shield Day. Monster High has never been so freaky-fab!

Rochelle Goyle

Rochelle is an exchange student all the way from Scaris. Like all gargoyles, she loves rules—keeping order is *très* important! And like any true Scarisian, Rochelle is always decked out in her favorite fashions, like Scaremès, Furberry, and Barks Macobs.

What else do you know about Rochelle?
Test yourself by filling in the blanks below!

1. Rochelle's freaky flaw is _____
   _____.

2. Her hair is ghoulgeous shades of ____
   _____
   and _____.

3. Rochelle's pet gargoyle griffin, _____
   _____, is always happy.

4. Her favorite snack is _____
   _____. *Très délicieux!*

5. She often cites rules from her favorite
   book, _____
   _____.

6. Rochelle's ex-boyfriend, _____
   _____, still lives in Scaris.

Ghoul Code

Rochelle loves to follow the rules in the Gargoyle Code of Ethics. Get together with your ghoulfriends to come up with your own list of rules to follow!

Paragraph 0.2:

A ghoul should never let a ghoulfriend go to the Maul alone.

Paragraph 0.9:

It is not safe to text on your iCoffin while crossing the street.

Paragraph 1.6:

_____

Paragraph 2.9:

_____

Paragraph 3.7:

_____

Paragraph 4.8:

_____

Paragraph 5.1:

_____

Paragraph 6.7:

_____

Robecca Steam

Robecca is a friendly and forgetful ghoul, and she steams up when she gets flustered. She always says "the cat's pajamas," and she loves using a typewriter and other old-timey inventions.

What else do you know about Robecca?
Fill in the blanks below to find out whether you are a Robecca expert!

1. Rochelle's pet penguin, _____ _____, gets grumpy.

2. Her flaw is _____ _____.

3. Robecca's friend Cy Clops has only one _____.

4. Her freaky-chic shoes have _____ _____ in them.

5. You can often find Robecca practicing _____.

6. Robecca's skin is made of _____ _____.

1. Penny; 2. her faulty internal clock; 3. eye,
4. rockets; 5. Skultimate Roller Maze; 6. copper

Flurry of Worry

ROBECCA WORRIES ABOUT BEING LATE, BUT HER GHOULFRIENDS
ALWAYS MAKE HER FEEL WAY BETTER! WHAT DO YOUR
GHOULFRIENDS DO TO CALM YOU DOWN WHEN YOU'RE UPSET?

8

AND WHAT DO YOU DO TO SOOTHE YOUR
BEAST GFF WHEN SHE IS STRESSED OUT?

Venus McFlytrap

Venus is a scary-chic planet-conscious ghoul. When she is upset, she sneezes pollens of persuasion—whoever is hit by the pollens suddenly agrees with Venus's point of view. Claw-some!

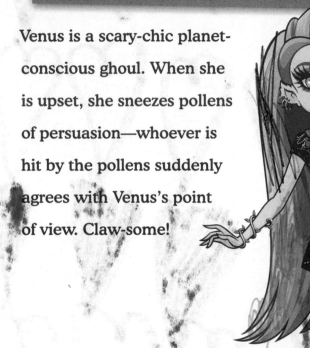

What else do you know about Venus?
Show off your insider info by completing
the sentences below.

1. Venus's father is the _____
   _____ monster.

2. Her pet, _____,
   loves metal and everything shiny.

3. Protecting the _____
   is very important to Venus.

4. She is good friends with _____,
   who also loves the planet.

5. Venus's favorite foods are _____
   _____
   and _____.

6. To change people's minds, Venus can
   use her _____.

Pollen PasSion

VENUS LOVES TAKING CARE OF THE PLANET! SHE TRIES TO HELP BY STARTING A COMPOST PILE, RECYCLING, AND TURNING OFF THE LIGHTS WHEN SHE LEAVES A ROOM. WHAT DO YOU DO TO HELP SAVE THE PLANET?

THE PLANET IS VENUS'S PASSION. WHAT ARE SOME THINGS YOU ARE PASSIONATE ABOUT? DO THEY INVOLVE SCHOOL? YOUR GHOULFRIENDS? SPOOKTACULAR HOBBIES? WRITE ABOUT THEM HERE!

NAME GAME

Some monsters are boarding students at Monster High, so instead of going home at the end of a ghouling school day, they stay in the dorms!

Rochelle, Venus, and Robecca's dorm room is called the Chamber of Gore and Lore. Some of the other dorm rooms are the Chamber of Ghoulery and Foolery, the Chamber of Tomb and Gloom, and the Chamber of Voltage and Moltage.

Get together with your ghoulfriends to come up with some spooktacular names for your own bedrooms! Use the scary-chic words from the sneak sheet on the right and think of some rhymes for them. Add your own words to the sneak sheet too! Then make a list of room names and pick your favorites!

Sneak Sheet

Chills _____

Claws _____

Delights _____

Fang _____

Fear _____

Freak _____

Fur _____

Madness _____

Scales _____

Scary _____

Snakes _____

Trolls _____

_____

_____

_____

_____

Chamber of _____

Chamber of _____

Chamber of _____

Chamber of _____

Chamber of _____

Chamber of _____

Chamber of _____

Chamber of _____

Chamber of _____

Chamber of _____

15

SKULTIMATE ROLLER MAZE

In **GHOULFRIENDS FOREVER**, Robecca signs up for Skultimate Roller Maze! Why does she love whooshing around on her rocket boots so much?

I am just wild about moving at super speeds. When I'm shooting around in my rocket boots, I don't even remember how forgetful I am!

SKULTIMATE SPORT

What sport are you beast at? Why do you think you're good at it? _____

_____

What sport do you think is the most fun? It might be different from the one you're beast at! What drives you wild about it? _____

_____

What sport is beast to play with your ghoulfriends?

_____

_____

Which Monster High sports team would you most want to be on? Why? _____

_____

SKULTIMATE EXIT

Robecca is caught deep in the maze.
Help her find her way out!

EXIT

19

MONSTER HIGH
MAZE MAKER

Now make some mazes of your own for your ghoulfriends to try to zoom through!

1. Using a pencil, outline a pathway along the grid from start to finish.

2. Let your pathway wind around the whole page so it won't be obvious that it's the correct path.

3. Include false pathways that lead to dead ends all through the maze.

4. To keep it freaky-fabulous, make some of the pathways move in swirls, stepladders, zigzags . . . let your imagination go wild!

START

FINISH

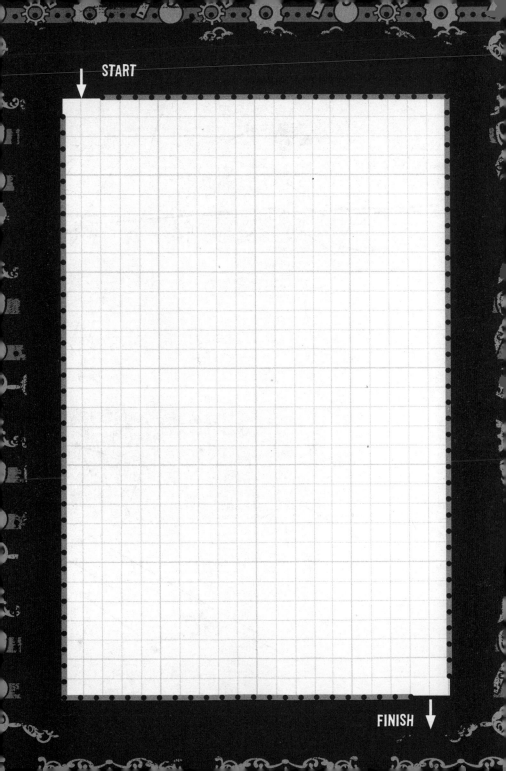

START

FINISH

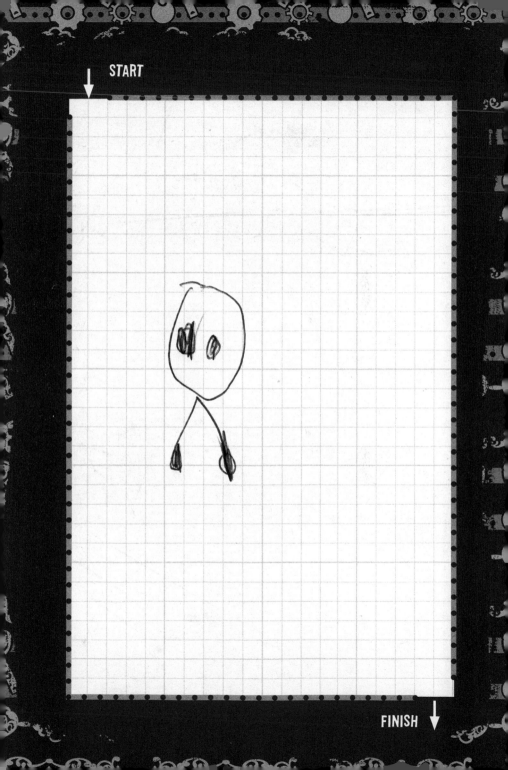

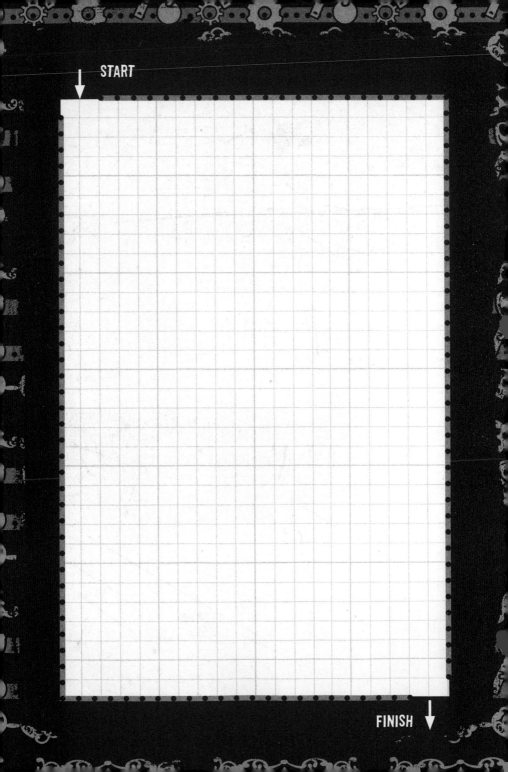

START

FINISH

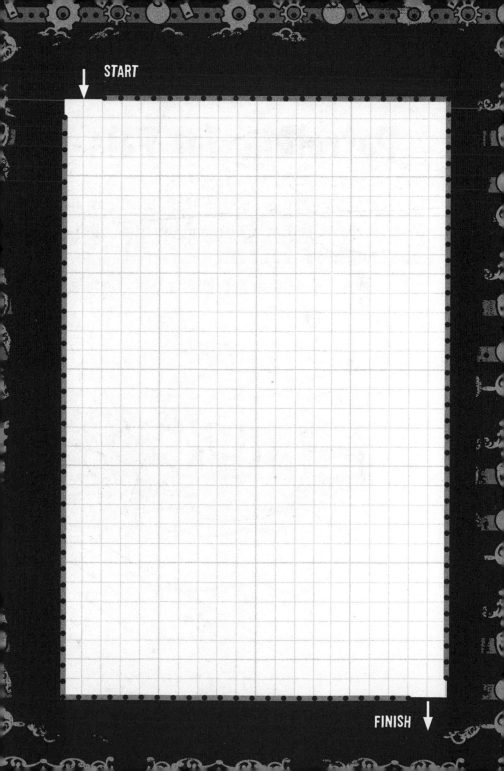

START

FINISH

Patrolling for Pals

The troll hall monitors seem a little hostile at first, but it turns out that trolls can be pals too—in **GHOULFRIENDS FOREVER**, one of them even tries to warn Venus that something bad is going to happen at Monster High.

GHOULFRIENDS FOR NEVER?

HOW DID YOU MEET EACH OF YOUR BEAST GHOULFRIENDS?

WHEN YOU MET YOUR BEASTIE, DID YOU KNOW RIGHT AWAY THAT YOU WOULD BE GHOULFRIENDS? WHY OR WHY NOT?

MONSTER HIGH BEASTIE

WHICH MONSTER HIGH STUDENT WOULD YOU LIKE TO BE BEAST GHOULFRIENDS WITH?

HOW DO YOU THINK YOU WOULD MEET HER?

WHAT WOULD YOU AND YOUR
MONSTER HIGH BEASTIE DO TOGETHER

WHICH OF YOUR GHOULFRIENDS SHARE SOME OF THE SAME PERSONALITY TRAITS AS YOUR BEAST MONSTER HIGH GHOUL?

Poems from Garrott

In **GHOULFRIENDS FOREVER**, Rochelle receives a DeadEx from her Scarisian then boyfriend, Garrott, with a poem inside. Receiving scale mail can be so much fun! Try writing some scary-cool poems for your ghoulfriends, then either mail them or deliver them in person.

Acreepstics

Normies call these poems *acrostics*, and they're claw-some! In an acreepstic, the first letters of the lines in the poem form a word, and the poem describes the word.

To make an acreepstic for one of your ghoulfriends, you can use her name or one of her favorite things.

34

Check out this poem for Venus:

*V*inetastic ghoulfriend

*E*nthusiastic about the environment

*N*eeds lots of sunshine

*U*nique monster

*S*cary-chic fashionista

On the next few pages, write an acreepstic for each of your ghoulfriends. You can also write them for your pet or about your favorite color, activity, season . . . the list goes on and on!

Acreepstics

_____   _____

_____   _____

_____   _____

_____   _____

_____   _____

_____   _____

_____   _____

_____   _____

_____   _____

_____   _____

_____   _____

_____   _____

_____   _____

Acreepstics

Sav

mom

Dbdy

Kauy

KA

A

H

37

Acreepstics

Hmom dog

A

Acreepstics

Designing for D'eath

In **GHOULFRIENDS FOREVER**, Rochelle wants to cheer Mr. D'eath up by rocking his wardrobe, and Frankie Stein and Clawdeen Wolf agree to help. Now the ghouls want to help you revamp your wardrobe too! Follow the steps below to get a Monster High makeover.

1. **PICK A STYLE.** DO YOU WANT TO BE SCARY SPORTY, WITH BATLETIC SHORTS AND SCARY-CUTE SNEAKS? SUPER CHIC, WITH GOLDEN JEWELS AND SKELEGANT GAUZE? GHOULISHLY GIRLY, WITH LOTS OF PINK AND BLACK LACE? HAUNTINGLY HIP, WITH ANIMAL PRINTS AND SAFETY PINS FOR DAYS? OR SOMETHING ELSE? DESCRIBE THE STYLE YOU'RE GOING FOR HERE:

_____

_____

_____

_____

2. CREEP YOUR CLOSET. PICK ALL THE CLOTHES THAT MATCH YOUR FUR–RAISING NEW STYLE AND EXPERIMENT WITH WHAT YOU ALREADY HAVE. REMEMBER TO INCLUDE ACCESSORIES TOO! LIST YOUR FAVE COMBOS HERE SO YOU DON'T FORGET THEM. (YOU CAN ALSO TAKE SELFIES OF YOUR SWEET STYLES, PRINT THEM OUT, AND GLUE THEM HERE.)

KILLER OUTFITS

3. CHECK OUT **TEEN SCREAM** AND YOUR OTHER FAVORITE MAGAZINES TO INSPIRE YOUR SEARCH FOR VERSATILE PIECES THAT CAN UPDATE YOUR WARDROBE—A SCAREDIGAN THAT CAN PAIR WITH JEANS OR A SKIRT, A SATINY SCARF THAT CAN ALSO WORK AS A BELT, A DRESS THAT CAN BE WORN WITH A BUTTON–DOWN OVER IT—AND GLUE OR LIST THOSE ITEMS HERE. THEN START SAVING YOUR CASH!

SCARY
KUTE

46

CREEPY COOL

MS. Mom

I LOl

GHOULFRIEND
UPDATE

Now that your own style is shiny, scaly, and new, help one of your ghoulfriends with hers!

1. PICK A STYLE FOR YOUR GHOULFRIEND.

2. CREEP HER CLOSET AND WRITE OR GLUE PICTURES OF THE BEAST COMBOS.

3. GO BACK TO **TEEN SCREAM**, THIS TIME KEEPING AN EYEBALL OUT FOR CLOTHES FOR YOUR GHOULFRIEND INSTEAD OF YOURSELF! GLUE OR LIST YOUR FAVES BELOW.

Haunted Happenings

Boo-la-la! Some *activités mystérieuses*, mysterious activities, are going on at Monster High. Ghouls who are usually outspoken or friendly are acting reserved and aloof. Teachers are changing their lesson plans. Unexplained objects are appearing in the halls. And everyone is strangely interested in Miss Flapper.

According to paragraph 213.8 of the Gargoyle Code of Ethics, it is the responsibility of all gargoyles to observe and track unusual occurrences in case they can discover clues that will help solve the case. So, *s'il ghoul plaît*, help Robecca, Venus, and me keep a record of the *activités étranges*, strange activities, that have been happening.

ROCK-SOLID
RECORD KEEPING

As you read **GHOULFRIENDS FOREVER** and the other books in the series, help keep track of the unusual goings-on at Monster High by writing an entry in the record book on the following pages each time any of these things happen:

 a student does something out of character

 a teacher or faculty member changes their plans

 anyone is seen talking to Miss Flapper

 anything unusual appears anywhere in the school

 any rumors start circulating

Write down who is involved, what happened, and what you think it means, and see if you can figure out what's going on!

_____

_____

_____

_____

_____

_____

_____

_____

_____

_____

_____

_____

_____

_____

r

ms.mom

53

TO ZAK
ZGWLOVE
YOU
YOU Are
THE

To lot
JON LOVE
you
SAYS
9:47

TO MOM
FROM
SAV
I LOVE
YOU

MONSTER HIGH

57

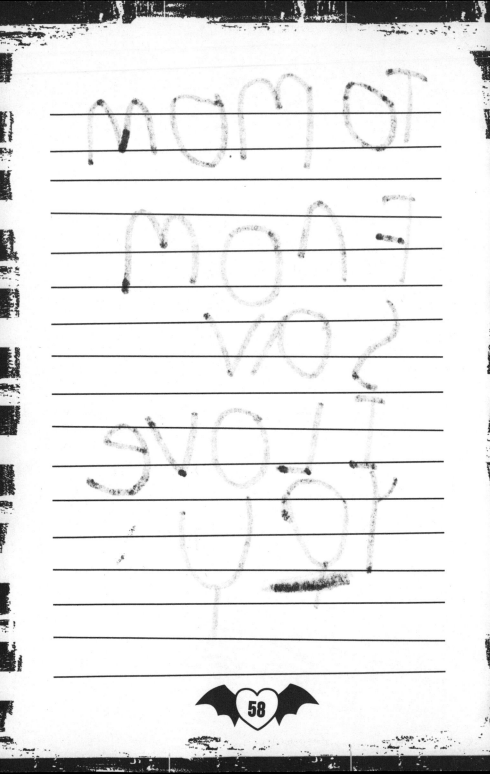

To Dad

From Sav

I Love

You

59

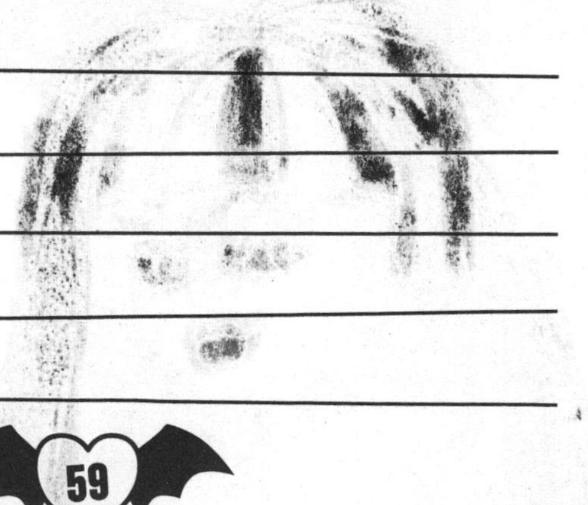

DANCE OF THE DELIGHTFULLY DEAD

Every year, Monster High has a Dance of the Delight-fully Dead, complete with a Scream Queen. Plan your own spooky school dance with your ghoulfriends!

a totally golden skelebration will have totally golden decorations! First, pick a freaky-fab theme for your dance. (I recommend making the whole thing desert-themed, but I'm just royalty, so what do I know?)

FRIGHT LIGHTS

WITH YOUR GHOULFRIENDS, MAKE A LIST OF THEME IDEAS,
THEN VOTE ON YOUR FAVORITES!

◇ _____   ◇ _____

◇ _____   ◇ _____

◇ _____   ◇ _____

NOW PICK A COLOR SCHEME. MONSTER HIGH'S COLORS OF PINK AND BLACK
ARE ALWAYS FREAKY-CHIC. WHAT OTHER COMBOS ARE TO DIE FOR?

◇ _____   ◇ _____

◇ _____   ◇ _____

◇ _____   ◇ _____

FINALLY, YOU NEED YOUR DECORATIONS! WILL YOU HAVE FLOCKS OF
CONSTRUCTION-PAPER BATS? PILES OF PAPIER-MÂCHÉ PYRAMIDS?
MONSTER HIGH BANNERS? ANIMAL-PRINT CREPE PAPER? MAKE A
LIST OF IDEAS, THEN DISCUSS HOW TO MAKE IT HAPPEN!

_____

_____

_____

SCREAM QUEEN

DRAW A SCARY-CHIC CROWN FOR THE SCREAM QUEEN HERE. INCLUDE
SPOOKTACULAR DETAILS, LIKE CLAW-SOME ZIPPERS OR ROT-IRON SWIRLS,
AND FINISH IT OFF BY GLUING ON SOME SEQUINS IN BOLD, WILD COLORS!

power play

CREATE A KILLER PLAYLIST FOR YOUR GHOULS TO GET DOWN TO!
NOTE YOUR FAVORITE TUNES HERE, AND UPDATE THE LIST WHEN
NEW SOUND WAVES MAKE A WILD SPLASH ON THE TOP 40.

★ _____
★ HADes
★ _____
★ _____
★ _____
★ _____
★ _____
★ _____
★ _____
★ _____
★ _____
★ _____
★ _____
★ _____
★ _____

FRIGHTFULLY FORGETFUL

NO ONE SEEMS TO REMEMBER WHAT HAPPENED AT SCHOOL LAST YEAR;
EVERYONE IS ACTING AS FORGETFUL AS HEADMISTRESS BLOODGOOD.
KEEP YOUR OWN MEMORY STRONG BY PLAYING THE GAMES BELOW!

MONSTER HIGH MADNESS

TALK WITH YOUR GHOULFRIENDS ABOUT MONSTER HIGH,
AND SEE IF YOU CAN REMEMBER WHAT EVERYONE SAYS!

INSTRUCTIONS:

1. Sit in a circle with your ghoulfriends.

2. Ghoul A says something about Monster High. For example,
   "Clawdeen's clothes are scary-cute!"

3. Ghoul B repeats what Ghoul A said, then adds her own statement:
   "Clawdeen's clothes are scary-cute! Deuce Gorgon loves to cook!"

4. Ghoul C repeats what Ghouls A and B said, then adds her own
   statement, and so on.

5. Keep going around the circle for as long as
   you can, then start a new round!

CHECK OUT
GHOULFRIENDS JUST
WANT TO HAVE FUN
TO FIND OUT WHETHER
EVERYONE REMEMBERS WHAT
REALLY HAPPENED.

COUNT FABULOUS'S COUNTDOWN

DRACULAURA'S PET BAT, COUNT FABULOUS, MAY BE SOPHISTICATED, BUT HE KNOWS HOW TO HAVE A GOOD TIME. HAVE SOME FANGTASTIC FUN WITH HIM AS YOU TRY TO REMEMBER WHERE YOU FALL IN THE COUNT.

INSTRUCTIONS:

1. Stand in a circle and pick one ghoul to be Little Bat.

2. Clockwise from Little Bat, assign numbers (in order) to the remaining ghouls. So if there are five ghouls, you'll have Little Bat, Number One, Number Two, Number Three, and Number Four.

3. Create a beat by slapping your hands against your legs at the same tempo.

4. To start a round, shout all together, "Oh, yeah! Little Bat, Little Bat, Little Bat!"

5. Little Bat starts the game by saying, "Little Bat," then another ghoul's number. The second ghoul says her number, then someone else's, and so on, like this:

   "Little Bat, Number Four!"
   "Number Four, Number Two!"
   "Number Two, Little Bat!"
   "Little Bat, Number One!"

HOT TIPS:

🦇 IF SOMEONE MAKES A MISTAKE, SHE MOVES TO THE END, AND EVERYONE'S NUMBERS CHANGE EXCEPT FOR LITTLE BAT'S. THEN YOU START A NEW ROUND.

🦇 IF LITTLE BAT MAKES A MISTAKE, SHE MOVES TO THE END, AND NUMBER ONE BECOMES LITTLE BAT.

🦇 ONCE YOU GET USED TO THE GAME, SEE HOW FAST YOU CAN GO!

frightingale society

Rochelle, Venus, and Robecca feel thrills and chills when they're invited to join the Frightingale Society, a sorority at Monster High devoted to community service and fostering life-and-death-long friendships between monsters. It's a huge honor to be asked to be a member!

ghouls' society

As one of the copresidents of the Frightingale Society, I might be biased, but I think it's voltageous! Building friendships with amazing ghouls and helping out your community is electrifying. You and your ghoulfriends should start a ghouls' society of your own!

WHAT WILL YOUR SOCIETY'S NAME BE?

_____

WHEN, WHERE, AND HOW OFTEN WILL YOU MEET?

_____

_____

LIST THE MEMBERS BELOW. REMEMBER, WHEN IT COMES
TO ASKING GHOULS TO JOIN A TOTALLY CLAW-SOME SOCIETY,
THE MORE THE SCARIER!

WHAT KINDS OF THINGS WILL YOU DO TOGETHER? WILL YOU WORK ON
PROJECTS? WILL YOU HAVE CREEPOVERS? WILL YOU TEACH ONE ANOTHER
SCARY-SWEET NEW SKILLS? WRITE DOWN ALL YOUR IDEAS!

67

project
scare and care

As the other copresident of the
Frightingale Society, I have seen that
one way to show ghoulfriends love is
by using your own boo-nique skills
and freaky flaws to help
one another out. After you
and your ghoulfriends
answer the questions
below, do some scaring
and caring of
your own!

Ghoulfriend #1

_____

Favorite things to do: _____

_____

Skills you have, based on your favorite things to do (if you love going to the Maul, you'd be a good fashion stylist; if you're batty for animals, you might be a great pet sitter): _____

_____

_____

Now pick your favorite skill, and write down some ways you could share it with your ghoulfriends and other monsters you know. (For example, if your skill is drawing, you could give lessons, draw pictures as gifts, or make greeting cards for your ghoulfriends to give to one another.) _____

_____

_____

Ghoulfriend #2

_____

Favorite things to do: _____

_____

_____

_____

Skills you have, based on your favorite things to do:

_____

_____

_____

Now pick your favorite skill, and write down some ways you could share it with your ghoulfriends and other monsters you know. _____

_____

_____

_____

_____

Ghoulfriend #3

_____

Favorite things to do: _____

~~I love you~~ Ms. Mom

Skills you have, based on your favorite things to do:

DARK

Now pick your favorite skill, and write down some ways you could share it with your ghoulfriends and other monsters you know. _____

_____

_____

_____

71

Ghoulfriend #4

_____

Favorite things to do: _____

_____

_____

Skills you have, based on your favorite things to do:

_____

_____

_____

Now pick your favorite skill, and write down some
ways you could share it with your ghoulfriends and
other monsters you know. _____

_____

_____

_____

_____

72

Ghoulfriend #5

_____

Favorite things to do: _____

_____

_____

_____

Skills you have, based on your favorite things to do:

_____

_____

_____

_____

Now pick your favorite skill, and write down some
ways you could share it with your ghoulfriends and
other monsters you know. _____

_____

_____

_____

_____

73

THE GREEN TEAM

Lagoona and Venus have joined together to save the environment for Project Scare and Care. They're working on a compost pile already, but they need your help with recycling!

A Wave of Recyclables

Say GDAY to the trash can and start sorting paper from plastic. My gills love clean water with no trash in it, and things you recycle won't end up in the ocean. You also keep landfills from being so full. And if you reuse things, you save money—which means it's easier to save up for new coral-studded platforms!

How else does recycling help?

- _____
- _____
- _____
- _____
- _____

There are all kinds of things you can do if you want to start recycling, or just recycle more. Add your own items to the list—and be as wild as you want!

- set up bins for paper, plastic, glass, and metal at your house and school
- gather recyclable materials from your neighbors
- reuse old things–transform a T-shirt into a throw pillow
- make necklaces out of soda can tabs
- turn old tin cans into rocket boots like Robecca's

- _____
- _____
- _____
- _____
- _____

Make a plan for putting your more realistic recycling ideas into action, mate! Write a letter to your scarents or teachers explaining what groovy thing you want to do, why you want to do it, and how you can participate every day in making it freaky-fabulous.

Dear _____,

NOW THAT YOUR RECYCLING PROJECT IS UNDER WAY, CHECK OUT HOW VENUS AND LAGOONA'S COMPOST PILE FARED IN **GHOULFRIENDS JUST WANT TO HAVE FUN**.

Monster Mash

When Lagoona and Venus start their compost pile, Toralei Stripe gives Venus a hard time about it, so the pollentastic plant monster makes up the word *mully* (monster + bully). Have a contest with your ghoulfriends to see who can make up the creepy-coolest word!

Write all your word combinations below. Use these examples as inspiration!

ghoul + beautiful = ghouliful

groovy + teacher = greacher

Monster Mash more words together . . .

DOLLS OF DOOM

In **GHOULFRIENDS JUST WANT TO HAVE FUN**, Robecca, Rochelle, and Venus find some dolls of doom in Catacombing class. Mr. Mummy explains that dolls of doom were given out by soothsayers as signs of bad luck to come. Rochelle isn't superstitious—but Robecca and Venus are!

Turn these dolls of doom into dolls of delight by giving them monster makeovers! Want to go wild? Draw some animal prints. Feeling royal? Glue on some claw-some sequins and rhinestones. Dying to look spooky-smart? Draw on a pair of creepy-chic glasses. Use your imagination!

LEISURE TREASURE

There are other creeptastic treasures buried in the catacombs, so keep digging to see what else you'll find.

Boo-la-la! You found a decorative hair clip shaped like a bat. Draw it here:

That gleam you just spotted is another ancient key—but this one is elaborate and encrusted with jewels. Draw it here:

Wild! You unearthed a long necklace made of everlasting flowers. Draw it here:

It looks as though the snake amulet you dug up may have belonged to one of Deuce's ancestors.

Draw it here:

GHOSTLY GOSSIP

AS MYSTERIOUS EVENTS UNFOLD AT MONSTER HIGH, SPECTRA VONDERGEIST KEEPS THE SCHOOL UP-TO-DATE VIA HER BLOG. SHE ALSO POSTS ABOUT ALL THE USUAL SUBJECTS: CREEPY-COOL FASHIONS, THE LATEST RUMORS, AND WHETHER THERE WILL BE A POP QUIZ IN G-OGRE-PHY (THERE WILL!).

Ghostly Gossip: Dressed to Kill

The most furrocious dresser at Monster High was spotted in a brand-new miniskirt today. Word on the screech is that she's looking to outshine everyone's favorite werecat. What do you wear when you want your fashion to be fearsome? Tell me all about your killer clothes in the comments section, ghouls!

COMMENTS:

Name:
Response:

Name:
Response:

Name:
Response:

Ghostly Gossip: Lit Fit

A certain Ghoulish Literature professor has been threatening to assign some major reading, and it looks like he's not bluffing, so brush off your copies of *Wuthering Frights*. What book would you most like to read for class? Creep all about it in the comments!

COMMENTS:

Name:
Response:

Name:
Response:

Name:
Response:

Ghostly Gossip: Spooky Storms

Umbrellas up, monsters! A storm system is thundering our way, and the weather will be frightful, unless rain is your cup of terror tea. (Confidential: A certain voltageous ghoul better stay inside—otherwise she might short out!) As for me, I find the howling winds comforting. What kind of weather do you like beast? Scare and share in the comments!

COMMENTS:

Name:
Response:

Name:
Response:

Name:
Response:

Ghostly Gossip: Rocky Romance

A certain stony fella might be having trouble with his fave mummy. The inseparable duo was spotted having a shouting match outside the Home Ick classroom. Here's hoping they make up! What do you do to make up with one of your friends when you've had an argument? Write your claw-some comments below!

COMMENTS:

Name:
Response:

Name:
Response:

Name:
Response:

WHITE AND WILD

In **GHOULFRIENDS JUST WANT TO HAVE FUN**, Monster High is overrun by white cats—which most monsters think are bad luck! Calm the student body down by giving these kitties some scary-sweet style and ghoulamorous accessories so they aren't solid white anymore.

USE A PURRFECT PLAID PATTERN TO GIVE THIS CREEPY–COOL KITTY SOME COLOR!

ADD SOME ROYAL SPARKLE TO THIS LITTLE CAT BY GLUING SOME GOLD SEQUINS ON HER AND DRAWING SOME MUMMY GAUZE AND A FEW AMULETS.

GIVE THIS KITTEN SOME CLAW–SOME MONSTERFIED RIBBONS AND BOWS TO BRIGHTEN HER UP!

SHOW THAT THIS ZOMBIE KITTY HAS BRAINS BY GIVING HER GLASSES AND A STACK OF MAD SCIENCE BOOKS.

MONSTERS THINK WHITE CATS ARE BAD LUCK—AND NORMIES THINK *BLACK* CATS ARE BAD LUCK! WHAT OTHER SUPERSTITIONS DO YOU KNOW ABOUT? WRITE THEM HERE!

Good luck

BAD LUCK

ROBECCA THINKS THE WHITE CATS ARE UNLUCKY. WHAT DO YOU THINK SHE WROTE IN HER JOURNAL THE DAY THE CATS STARTED TO APPEAR?

Dear Diary,

zak

eronuf

HEX FACTOR TALON SHOW

In **GHOULFRIENDS JUST WANT TO HAVE FUN**, Cleo de Nile and Toralei are in charge of the talent show, and they need your help to make it freaky-fabulous!

The scream of the crop at Monster High all want to show that they're the cat's meow, but some of the students are having trouble deciding which of their claw-some talents to display. Help them out with some furrocious ideas!

Purrfect Performance

LAGOONA BLUE: _____

_____

HOLT HYDE: _____

_____

101

ROBECCA STEAM: _____

_____

CLAWDEEN WOLF: _____

_____

CATTY NOIR: _____

_____

DRACULAURA: _____

_____

KILLER ACT

IF YOU WANT TO BE IN MONSTER HIGH'S HEX FACTOR TALON SHOW TOO, YOU'LL NEED TO PUT TOGETHER A THRILLING PERFORMANCE. GET READY TO MAKE THE CROWD SHRIEK, "OH MY RA!"

WHAT HAVE YOU ALWAYS DREAMED OF DOING IN FRONT OF A RA-DORING AUDIENCE? JUGGLING GOLDEN BANGLES? SINGING? JUGGLING GOLDEN BANGLES *WHILE* SINGING? WRITE DOWN ALL YOUR IDEAS!

PICK YOUR FAVORITE IDEA (OR COMBINATION OF IDEAS) AND WRITE DOWN SOME DETAILS, LIKE WHETHER YOU WILL NEED MUSIC OR PROPS. IF YOUR IDEA IS FOR A DUO, TRIO, OR BIGGER GROUP, MAKE SURE TO INCLUDE YOUR GHOULFRIENDS IN THE PLANNING.

DO YOU NEED TO LEARN THE LYRICS TO A SONG, WRITE A MONOLOGUE, OR CHOREOGRAPH A DANCE TO MAKE YOUR PERFORMANCE HAPPEN? CREATE A GAME PLAN!

NOW FOR THE FINISHING TOUCH: PUTTING TOGETHER A CREEPERIFIC COSTUME! DESCRIBE YOUR SCARY-CHIC ENSEMBLE.

DEADLY DECOR

In **WHO'S THAT GHOULFRIEND?**, Robecca, Rochelle, and Venus find Wydowna Spider's webbed room—and the decorations are ghoulgeous. Dream up your own silky-sweet room decor here, then use it as a guide for a remodel.

To spin a chic and cozy web, start by listing what you love about your room! Is your bedding to live for? Are your walls a defrightful hue? Do you have the perfect wastebasket next to your desk? Write about your favorite pieces here.

_____

_____

THE BEAST ROOMS HAVE A FLY COLOR SCHEME. WHAT COLORS WOULD YOU LIKE TO SEE WHEN YOU WAKE UP IN THE MOANING?

_____

_____

YOUR FURNITURE CAN BE COZY, CHIC, OR BOTH. WHAT IS YOUR
CURRENT FURNITURE STYLE, AND WHAT WOULD YOU CHANGE IT TO?
ROCHELLE WOULD LOVE FURNITURE THAT LOOKED LIKE
IT BELONGED TO MARIE FANGTOINETTE!

_____

_____

_____

_____

LET'S TALK DETAILS! ARE YOU A FANGED FAN OF FIGURINES, OR DO YOU
PREFER POSTERS? DO YOU WANT CROCHETED SHAWLS DRAPING EVERY
SURFACE? LAMPS IN EVERY OPEN SPACE? FRAMED PORTRAITS OF CATTY
NOIR AND BONE DIRECTION? WRITE ABOUT EVERYTHING FROM RUGS
TO THROW PILLOWS TO GET A GOOD SENSE OF WHAT YOU'D LOVE.

_____

_____

_____

_____

Webbed Wonder

DRAW A PICTURE OF YOUR THREADFULLY COOL DREAM ROOM,
JUST THE WAY YOU WANT IT TO BE!

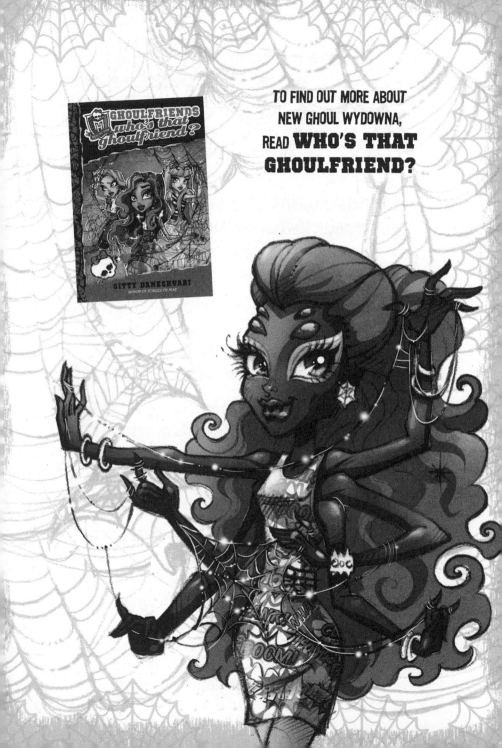

TO FIND OUT MORE ABOUT
NEW GHOUL WYDOWNA,
READ **WHO'S THAT
GHOULFRIEND?**

FANGTASTIC ROOMMATES
THE GRAPHIC NOVEL

KEEP YOUR GHOULFRIENDS UP-TO-DATE ON THE LATEST NEWS
FROM ROCHELLE, REBECCA, AND VENUS BY WRITING A SCENE
FROM A GRAPHIC NOVEL FOR THEM TO READ.

HOT TIPS:

Write lightly in pencil so it's easy to change things. When
you're completely finished, go over all the dialogue in pen.

Thought balloons are connected to the speaker's head with a
line of circles. Speech balloons are connected to the speaker's
mouth with an arrow. Sound bursts look like little explosions.
And long, rectangular strips are used to indicate the passage
of time.

Let the ghouls have a real conversation where they listen and
respond to one another, but also give each ghoul a primary
focus. Maybe Rochelle is thinking about a new ensemble for
Mr. D'eath, Venus needs help with new composting ideas, and
Rebecca forgot Penny somewhere.

Allow at least one piece of the conversation to resolve by the last panel. If Rochelle can't find her new turtle-quoise belt in the first panel, maybe she finds out in the last panel that Chewlian ate it.

Practice saying the dialogue out loud. Does it sound like something you would say? If not, tweak it until it sounds natural.

Once the dialogue sounds good, you can add in some scary-cool Monster High language!

SAMPLE PAGE

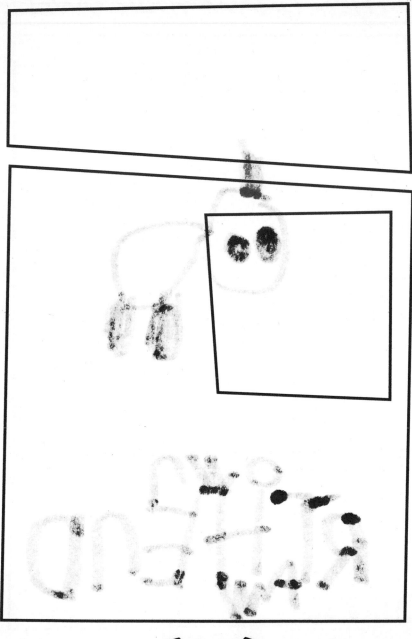

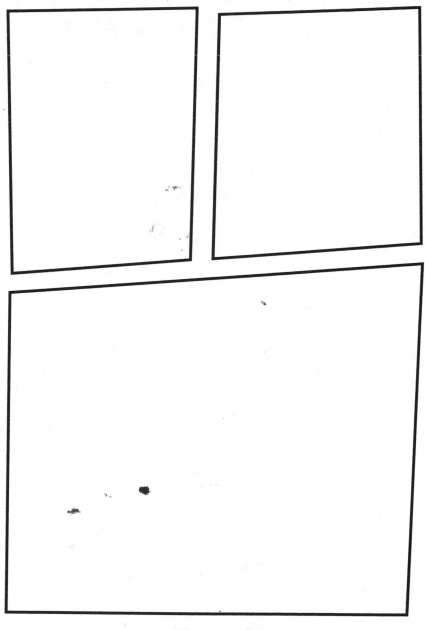

CHAIN OF EVENTS

In **WHO'S THAT GHOULFRIEND?**, there are some wild things going on at Monster High, so Cleo and Toralei take to walking around with their arms linked for security purposes—and a few cat-and-mummy fights ensue! That's a lot of time to spend with one other ghoul.

WHAT WOULD BE THE BEAST THING ABOUT BEING CHAIN-LINKED TO ONE OF YOUR GHOULFRIENDS?

_____

_____

_____

_____

WHAT WOULD BE THE MOST DIFFICULT THING?

_____

_____

_____

_____

WHICH OF YOUR SCARY—COOL GHOULS WOULD YOU MOST
WANT TO BE ATTACHED TO, AND WHY?

_____

_____

_____

_____

IF YOU WERE LINKED TO ONE OF YOUR BEASTIES, HOW WOULD YOU
COORDINATE YOUR OUTFITS? IDENTICAL, COMPLEMENTARY, OPPOSITE,
FAMOUS COUPLES . . . THERE ARE SO MANY OPTIONS!

_____

_____

_____

_____

WHAT IF ONE LINKED GHOUL WANTED TO PLAY CASKETBALL AND THE
OTHER WANTED TO GO TO THE LIBURY? HOW WOULD YOU WORK IT OUT?

_____

_____

_____

_____

Terrorific Tunes

When someone at Monster High goes missing in **WHO'S THAT GHOULFRIEND?**, Operetta writes a song to cheer everyone up. Try writing some songs of your own—happy ghouls can be made happier with a good song!

USE THESE TIPS TO CREATE A MONSTERIFIC MELODY:

FOR VERSES 1, 2, AND 4: RHYME THE FIRST THREE LINES OF EACH VERSE, AND USE THE SAME LINE 4 FOR EACH VERSE.

FOR VERSE 3: RHYME LINES 1 AND 3, AND RHYME LINES 2 AND 4.

SING EACH SONG YOU WRITE TO THE TUNE OF A SONG YOU KNOW, OR MAKE UP YOUR OWN TUNE! EXPERIMENT AND HAVE SOME PHANTASMIC FUN!

Here's a sample song:

VERSE 1:

Bring on another sunny day.
Monsters want to dance and play.
We have always been this way.
Monster High will rock, rock.

VERSE 2:

Play another cheerful song.
Ghosts and vamps will sing along.
We are sassy, sweet, and strong.
Monster High will rock, rock.

VERSE 3:

Listen to that killer beat.
This party is spooktacular.
Wave your hands and stomp your feet.
That's my kind of vernacular.

VERSE 4:

Bring it back into the halls.
Party when you're at the Maul.
Fun for one and fun for all—
Monster High will rock, rock.

VERSE 1:

_____
_____
_____
_____
_____

VERSE 2:

_____
_____
_____
_____
_____

VERSE 3:

_____
_____
_____
_____
_____

VERSE 4:

_____
_____
_____
_____
_____

VERSE 1:

_____

_____

_____

_____

VERSE 2:

_____

_____

_____

_____

VERSE 3:

_____

_____

_____

_____

VERSE 4:

_____

_____

_____

_____

PASSION FOR FASHION

Clawdeen makes a freaky-fly T-shirt for the ghouls in the Frightingale Society to wear to show support for Monster High's missing headmistress. Being chic for a cause is so in!

Make a list of some causes you could support with a T-shirt design. Whether you want to save the planet, save the polar bears, or just get a later curfew, you can design a shirt for it!

_____
_____
_____
_____
_____
_____
_____
_____

Now pick your favorite causes and start designing! You can use colored pencils, sequins, animal-print ribbons, wild-colored duct tape, and anything else you have on hand to make your designs come to life on the following pages.

Picture Day

When picture day comes to Monster High, every ghoul wants to look her beast. Check out Miss Flapper's tips on how to make picture day a success!

- *Practice your smile at home the night before so you know the beast way to show off those pearly whites.*

- *If it makes you feel more confident, give yourself a clawdicure the night before, even though your claws won't show in the picture.*

- *Wear bright, bold colors. Get together with your ghoulfriends the weekend before to pick out all your most claw-some outfits.*

- *When it comes to your furstyle, go with classic and chic.*

- *Bring a small mirror with you so you can check that your hair and scales are all in place. (If you're a vampire, just ask a friend how you look!)*

- *Tilt your chin up just a smidge for the photographer and flash that smile you practiced!*

Scary-Sweet Selfies

Do a picture-day practice run by breaking out the digital camera and shooting some selfies. Pick a claw-some backdrop, use natural light if you can, and add a filter to the image—sepia is always a golden bet! Print out and glue your pharaohific pics on the following pages.

A BIG SECRET IS REVEALED ON PICTURE DAY IN WHO'S THAT GHOULFRIEND? READ THE BOOK TO FIND OUT WHAT IT IS!

Selfie File

Selfie File

CRACK AND SHIELD DAY

At Monster High's groovy end-of-year athletic competition, Venus competes in the Ghoul's Cry Jump (which is sort of like a normie high jump, but you have to shriek while you do it).

What other events might take place at Monster High's Crack and Shield Day? With your ghoulfriends, come up with some possibilities by giving normie sports and games a monster twist! Add your ideas to the list below.

 TROLL HERDLES (A RACE WHERE YOU HAVE TO JUMP OVER HERDS OF MOVING TROLLS)

 LEG-AND-SPOON RACE (A PARTNER RACE WHERE **GHOUL A** HOLDS A SPOON AND **GHOUL B** HOLDS HER LEG OVER THE SPOON AND HOPS ON HER OTHER FOOT)

_____

_____

_____

_____

CRACK AND SHIELD TROPHY

Even Miss Sue Nami, the school's strict Deputy of Disaster, can agree that non-adult entities who succeed at competitive sporting events deserve a spooktacular reward. Design a trophy that shows off the style and substance of this venerable educational institution.

PeT PRoJeCT

IN **GHOULFRIENDS 'TIL THE END**, VENUS, ROBECCA,
AND ROCHELLE BRING THEIR PETS WITH THEM AS THEY SEARCH THE
SCHOOL FOR CLUES ABOUT THE MYSTERIOUS HAPPENINGS.

HOW DO YOU INCLUDE YOUR OWN PETS IN YOUR DAILY UNLIFE?
DO YOU TAKE THEM TO THE MAUL? DO YOU PLAY WITH THEM OUTSIDE?
DO YOU SNUGGLE WITH THEM? WRITE ABOUT ALL THE WAYS
YOU HANG OUT WITH YOUR PET!

making pets with pencils

Learn to draw using Penny as
a monster pet model!

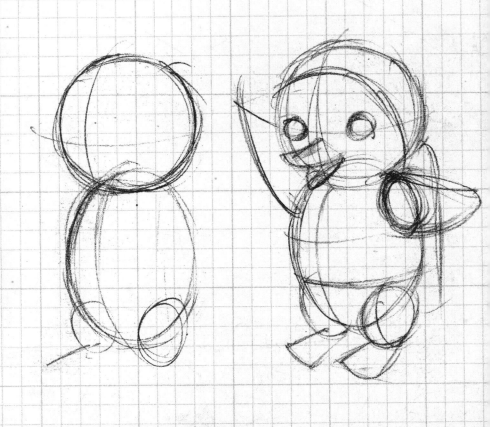

Start with basic body shapes, then add
shapes for Penny's flippers and beak.
Draw in her helmet and jet pack, and then
finish with shading and details!

Practice drawing
Penny!

138

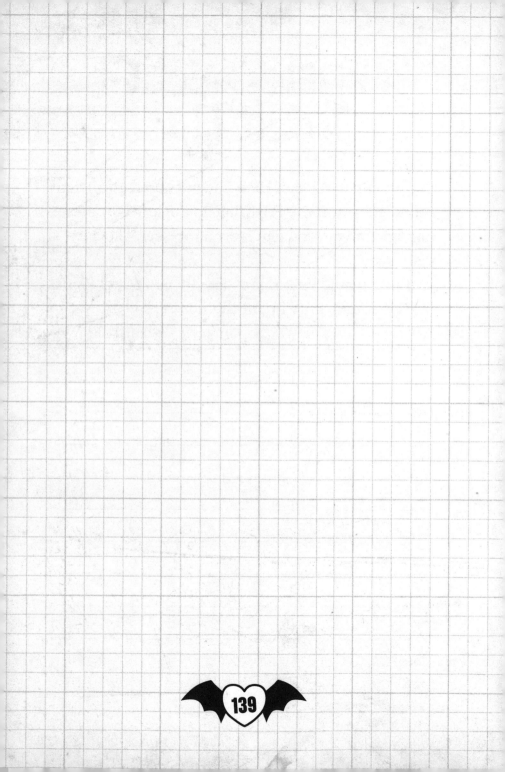

SUPER SECRET SOCIETY

The ghouls at Monster High find out about an ancient secret society. If the Frightingale Society isn't secret enough for you, you can start a top secret society of your own.

What would your secret society be about? Pick a few ideas and write about them here.

_____

_____

_____

_____

_____

_____

_____

_____

_____

_____

How would you identify
society members?
I think a pyramid-
shaped amulet would
be killer, but you could
all wear gold ribbons,
or mummy gauze, or
chic headbands—the
possibilities are endless!
Come up with a list of
ideas, then pick your
favorites.

_____
_____
_____
_____
_____
_____
_____
_____

JINAFIRE LONG IS KNOWN FOR HER CLAW-SOME DESIGN SKILLS.
LIGHT THE FIRES OF CREATIVITY AND DO SOME DESIGNING OF YOUR OWN:
DRAW A SCARY-COOL LOGO FOR YOUR SECRET SOCIETY!

Society Code

According to paragraph 87.4 of the Gargoyle Code of Ethics, *sociétés secrètes*, secret societies, are required to have a list of rules and regulations in order to avoid anarchy and chaos. Rochelle began a list of *très* useful rules; add some of your own.

 You must have a <u>fangtastique</u> talking diamonster (or other gem). When a ghoul is holding the diamonster, it is her turn to talk.

 Ghouls should look their beast at meetings. This shows your fellow members that you respect them.

 You may never show anyone your society's secret handshake. (Related: You must create a secret handshake!)

FOR MORE ON THE MONSTERS'
SECRET SOCIETIES, READ
GHOULFRIENDS
'TIL THE END.

Spider Style

With her weaving skills, Wydowna is a queen spider when it comes to fashion, and she can sense what your personal style is. With your ghoulfriends, take this quiz to find out which Monster High ghoul's style is most like your own.

1. Which colors do you most like to rock?
   a. scary-chic pastels
   b. bright attention-grabbing shades
   c. any colors from a metallic palette
   d. warm oranges and reds

2. Which kinds of accessories do you like beast?
   a. chic metal bracelets and tiaras
   b. anything with fangtastic flowers
   c. creepy-cool mechanical parts made into jewelry
   d. bracelets—lots and lots of bracelets

3. Which freaky fabric is your favorite?
   a. something smooth and classic
   b. all-natural fibers
   c. anything with some shimmer
   d. freaky-chic lace

4. How do you like to style your hair?
   a. every hair in place
   b. something funky and unexpected
   c. wild and free
   d. full of body but still silky smooth

5. Which word beast describes you?
   a. romantic
   b. outspoken
   c. adventurous
   d. imaginative

Fill in your answers here!

Name	Question 1	Question 2	Question 3	Question 4	Question 5

 If you chose mostly **A**s, you and **Rochelle Goyle** have the same style! You both love classic, timeless looks with scary-chic twists.

 If you chose mostly **B**s, you and **Venus McFlytrap** have the same style! You dress to impress—and to draw attention—in colors and styles as bold as you are.

 If you chose mostly **C**s, you and **Robecca Steam** have the same style! You are both retro and edgy, and you love to work the metallic look.

 If you chose mostly **D**s, you and **Wydowna Spider** have the same style! Lacy and skelegant, but still totally scary-cool—with lots of silky red touches.

Silk Threads

Wydowna loves to design clothes for other ghouls. Are you ready for a threadful new wardrobe?

Help her design a ruffled lace skirt for you. One ruffle is flirty, and lots of ruffles are punky—draw whichever one you prefer!

Silk Threads

No ghoul's wardrobe is complete without a claw-some patterned top. Whether you love plaids, stripes, geometric designs, animal prints, or something else, you can come up with a spooktacular pattern. Add your designs to these chic shirts!

150

151

Silk Threads

A ghoul's platforms are her beast friends. Draw your perfect pair here. Flowers, webs, rot iron—you have a lot of options.

Silk Threads

Finish off your brand-boo look with a super fly purse. An oversize hobo bag can hold everything you need for a day, and a clutch is perfect for partying with the ghouls. Draw something in the size and style that is beast for you!

THE MORE MONSTER YOU KNOW

Think you know everything about Monster High ghoulfriends? Take this quiz to find out!

1. What is the name of Headmistress Bloodgood's pet?

    _____

2. What happens when Operetta sings live?

    _____

3. What town is next to Monster High?

    _____

4. Who teaches Ghoulish Literature?

    _____

5. Where do Rochelle, Robecca, Venus, and Cy find the blueprints for the school?

    _____

6. Which ghouls are the copresidents of the Frightingale Society?

———————————————

7. Where do the Van Sangre sisters sleep?

———————————————

8. Who is the editor of Monster High's Fearbook?

———————————————

If you answered 1–2 questions correctly, you have some studying to do! If you answered 3–4 questions correctly, you need some work. If you answered 5–6 questions correctly, you're rock solid. If you answered 7–8 questions correctly, you're a Monster High ghoulfriends expert!

1. a horse named Nightmare; 2. listeners lose their minds for a few days; 3. Salem; 4. Dr. Clamdestine; 5. the Crybrary; 6. Frankie and Draculaura; 7. everywhere, because they're gypsies; 8. Toralei!

155

FACT ATTACK

If you're as forgetful as I am, you may have trouble remembering everything about your ghoulfriends. See how well you know them now. Each ghoul will make up her own quiz by writing questions about herself and then reading the questions aloud. See which of your beast buddies can guess the correct answer first. Ghould luck!

Quiz About _____

    1.

    2.

    3.

    4.

Quiz About _____

    1.

    2.

    3.

    4.

Quiz About _____

    1.

    2.

    3.

    4.

Quiz About _____

    1.

    2.

    3.

    4.

Sherlock Bones

So many mysterious things have been happening at Monster High! They have inspired me to use my love of creative biting to pen a mystery story as an extra-credit assignment for Dr. Clamdestine. You can earn extra credit too if you write a mystery story of your own!

HOT TIPS:

- Get ideas from the world around you ("The Case of the Missing iCoffin") or from a newspaper ("The Case of the Bad Bank Robber").

- Before you start writing, decide how the story's going to end, then write an outline in reverse order. (So you'll start your outline at the end of the story and work your way back to the beginning.) This way, your plot will make sense.

- Make up a freaktacular main character with a well-rounded personality. Your main character will also be your detective!

- Give your detective a beast friend and a few enemies.

- As your detective finds clues, show them to the reader. The detective shouldn't know anything the reader doesn't know.

- You can be serious or silly, complex or simple. Just have fun!

It was a dark and stormy night, and

Now that you've finished your first mystery story, you're a regular Ed-grrr Allan Poe. If you had fun writing, don't stop! Write another story starring the same detective, or start over with a whole new cast of characters. Happy writing!

163

Zombie Dance

Get down in slow motion with a funky zombie dance. And after you and your ghoulfriends each make up your own dance, have a zombie dance-off!

Here are a couple of different methods you can try to come up with your dance. But first, put on a song with a banging beat!

Brainy Moves

- WAVE YOUR ARMS IN THE AIR IN A TOTALLY WILD WAY FOR TWO BEATS.

- STRIKE A ZOMBIE POSE FOR TWO BEATS.

- MOVE YOUR LEGS AROUND IN A TOTALLY BOO-NIQUE WAY FOR TWO BEATS.

- STRIKE ANOTHER ZOMBIE POSE (OR THE SAME ONE!) FOR TWO BEATS.

- LATHER, RINSE, REPEAT!

Dead Wacky

- SHAKE YOUR WHOLE BODY AROUND FOR FOUR BEATS.

- PUMP YOUR ARMS IN THE AIR FOR FOUR BEATS.

- AND REPEAT!

What else can you do to create a defrightful dance?
Write some ideas here!

Zombie Dance-Off

PUT YOUR DANCING SHOES ON AND HAVE A KILLER CONTEST!

- FIRST CRANK UP THE MUSIC YOU CHOREOGRAPHED YOUR DANCES TO AND SET IT ON REPEAT.

- THEN STAND IN A CIRCLE AND MOVE TO THE BEAT.

- WITH EVERYONE STILL GROOVING IN THE CIRCLE, GHOUL A MOVES TO THE CENTER AND SHOWS OFF HER MOVES.

- WHEN GHOUL A IS FINISHED, GHOUL B TAKES THE CENTER, AND SO ON, UNTIL EVERYONE HAS GONE.

- NOW RECORD YOUR VOTES ON THE NEXT PAGE FOR BEAST RHYTHM, MOST BOO-NIQUE MOVES, AND BEAST OVERALL. BUT DON'T FORGET THAT IN A ZOMBIE DANCE-OFF, EVERYONE IS REALLY A WINNER!

166

Zombie Dance-Off Voting Central

NAME	BEAST RHYTHM	MOST BOO-NIQUE MOVES	BEAST OVERALL

Draw Your Ghoulfriends
Sketch Rochelle!

Start with a basic body outline, then
layer on shapes for her clothes, hair, and wings.

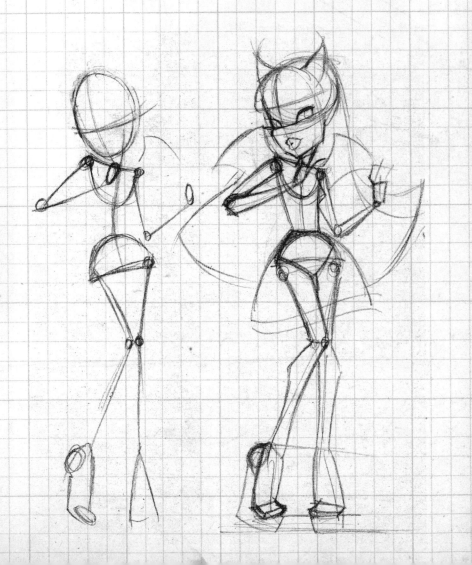

Draw a more solid outline and sketch in her
features before finishing with shading and details.

Draw Your Ghoulfriends
Sketch Robecca!

Start with a basic body outline, then
layer on shapes for her body, skirt, and hair.

Draw a more solid outline and sketch in her
features before finishing with shading and details.
Don't forget her goggles!

K.I.T. WITH THE GHOULS

It's been creeptastic hanging out with the ghouls of Monster High! But it isn't over—keep in touch with Robecca, Rochelle, Venus, and their friends, and check out **GHOULFRIENDS FOREVER** and the other books in the series to find out all the details of the mysteries they've been solving.

Already read about the ghoulfriends' creep-erific adventures saving Monster High from certain doom? Wondering what happens next? Will Rochelle ever stop quoting rules from the Gargoyle Code of Ethics? Will Venus ever tame her jewelry-munching pet, Chewlian? Does Robecca ever find her long-lost father, mad scientist Hexiciah Steam? Find out in this exclusive short story! Just turn the page!

(Haven't read the other books yet? Don't bolt—this story will still be a fangtastic read!)

GHOULFRIENDS

creep around the clock

A NEW SHORT STORY BY
GITTY DANESHVARI

If this guy wakes up, we're ghosts," Venus McFlytrap muttered as she, Robecca Steam, and Rochelle Goyle slipped their fingers into the dark and cavernous mouth of a slumbering beast.

The bearded dragon (and this is a literal description, as the elderly creature had an abundance of coarse white facial hair) released rattle-like snores as the ghouls investigated his unusually sharp teeth.

"Ghosts? I cannot say that I concur with that assessment," Rochelle responded quickly. "However, missing a limb? Most definitely."

"If only we had invited Wydowna Spider. With six arms, it wouldn't matter so much if she lost one," Robecca tried to joke as steam pumped ferociously out of her ears.

By now, you must be wondering how three upstanding ghouls without even the faintest history of dental training found themselves mining a soot-stained mouth for the key to a long-buried mystery. Well, it all began that morning, at sunrise to be exact. . . .

A warm, yellowish light cascaded down through the grove of conifurs and reflected off Robecca's copper-plated frame while she jetted between the trees.

Robecca had awoken suddenly, overwhelmed by a sense that she was late. Not a little bit late, not very late, but "I just missed half the day" late. With adrenaline pumping, she jumped out of bed and stormed down the hall before pausing to look out a window. A dark, star-littered sky greeted Robecca, resulting in a long and laborious sigh. As so often happened, she was *really early* instead of *really late*. But since she was already up, Robecca decided to flip on her rocket boots and take a quick spin around campus. Now, this was a ghoul with absolutely no understanding of time, so Robecca had to gauge her return by the colors in the sky. And the shift from yellow to pink was her cue to head back to the dormitory.

A soft jingling sound, similar to keys rattling on a chain, grabbed Robecca's attention as she made her way down one of Monster High's deserted corridors.

"Deary me! Is that you, Penny? Did I forget you

in the hall again? Whatever is the matter with me? Why can I never seem to remember where I put you? If only you'd learn to use an iCoffin, then you could call me," Robecca babbled while she looked around for her mechanical pet penguin.

But there wasn't a ghoul, monster, or creature in sight. *It must be time for a tune-up*, Robecca quickly deduced, and then continued on her way. And though the noise persisted, she paid it no mind, sure that it was nothing more than a loose screw knocking against one of her copper plates.

"Good morning, ghoulfriends!" Robecca hollered, bursting into the Chamber of Gore and Lore and instantly rousing her roommates, Rochelle Goyle and Venus McFlytrap.

"*Boo-la-la*, Chewy kept me up all night chomping on heaven knows what!" Rochelle moaned before throwing a disgruntled look at

Venus's pet plant on the windowsill.

"Sorry about that . . . and about your purple earrings. I'm pretty sure that's what he was noshing on," Venus admitted, then stood to give Chewy his morning shower.

"That plant is an absolute menace to accessories! Croako Chanel's worst nightmare," Rochelle stated with a huff before narrowing her eyes and tilting her head to concentrate.

"Look, I said—"

"Shhh!" Rochelle hushed Venus as she made her way across the room. "*Pardonnes-moi*, Venus, but I believe someone is at our door."

"But I was just in the hall, and there wasn't a soul in sight," Robecca mumbled.

"*C'est très bizarre; il n'y a personne.* There's no one here," Rochelle said upon opening the door and noting the empty corridor.

"Well, I didn't hear anything, so maybe you imagined it. Although, having said that, gargoyles aren't really known for their imaginations," Venus responded while wiping the sleep from her eyes.

"We are admittedly an analytical, logic-based bunch," Rochelle acquiesced. Then she saw something move out of the corner of her eye.

Slithering along the floor of the hallway, merely an inch from her pink slippers, was a pale blue cobra adorned head to tail in gold jewelry.

"It's Hissette, Cleo's snake," Rochelle announced to the others.

"She's probably looking for a refuge from listening to Cleo talk about herself nonstop," Venus joked.

Seconds later, the snake began to cough, her whole body writhing back and forth.

"*Ne t'inquiete pas*! Don't worry! I am well versed in administering the Grimelich maneuver to reptiles as well as monsters," Rochelle announced, and then pushed up her sleeves in preparation.

"Hold up, Dr. Goyle, I don't think that's going to be necessary," said Venus as she watched the snake drop a small scroll from her mouth.

"What a pain it must be not to have pockets! This poor snake has nowhere to carry anything except her mouth," Robecca fussed while Venus bent down and picked up the tiny scroll seconds before Hissette slithered away.

FROM THE TOMB OF
PRINCESS CLEO DE NILE

Dear Rebecca, Rochelle, and Venus,

I must speak with you ghouls immediately! As in fright now!

Actually, on second thought, let's make it 8:30 am in the Study Howl—a princess's beauty routine should never be rushed, not even when you're as gorgeous as I am.

Your royally fashionable highness,

Cleo de Nile

"Monsterful moss! I think Cleo is throwing herself another surprise birthday party. This is getting out of hand. It will be the fourth one this term," Venus mused, shaking her head.

"And her actual birthday still isn't for another seven months," Rochelle added.

"She better not expect another present, because three birthday gifts is my limit! Okay, fine, four is my limit. But that's it!" Rochelle grumbled while she closed the door to the Chamber of Gore and Lore.

But as Robecca, Rochelle, and Venus would soon learn, a surprise birthday party was the last thing on Cleo's mind. Okay, perhaps not the last thing, but definitely not the first.

Later that morning as vampires, zombies, and

werewolves trudged down the purple-checkered halls for the start of another day at Monster High, Robecca, Rochelle, and Venus headed to the Study Howl to meet Cleo de Nile.

"Move it, non-adult entities! Ma'am is coming through!" Miss Sue Nami, the school's Deputy of Disaster, barked as she cleared a path for Headmistress Bloodgood.

"Good morning, students! Rise and shine, but never rise and whine!" Headmistress Bloodgood announced while Rochelle, Venus, and Robecca exited the corridor.

"Cleo can't be serious. Is she really just sitting and staring at herself in a mirror?" Venus scoffed upon entering the Study Howl.

"When Cy Clops gets back from visiting his grandmother, you should ask him about his theory on Cleo. He thinks she's focusing on herself more than usual so she doesn't have to think about her father's disappearance," Robecca explained, gazing across the room at the always immaculately groomed mummy.

Almost three months had passed since Ramses de Nile had fled Salem after being exposed as a member of the Ancient Society of Monster Elite (ASOME)—a dangerous organization that adhered to a strict monster hierarchy, wherein vampires, mummies, and aristocratic ghosts were considered superior to other monsters. However, the royal mummy's offenses were not limited to his membership in ASOME. Far worse than simply being a part of ASOME's plan to bring Salem under its control was that he was also masquerading as a member of the Society of United Monsters (SUM)—a group dedicated to stopping ASOME. Ramses's life as a double agent had only been uncovered one other time in history—by Robecca's own father, Hexiciah Steam. And no one had seen Hexiciah since.

"Don't you ever get tired of looking at yourself?" Venus asked Cleo as the trio approached her table in the Study Howl.

"No way! And I highly doubt anyone else does either," Cleo replied, then dabbed her lips with a shimmery gold gloss.

"This is just a suggestion, but maybe you should find a hobby," Robecca offered genuinely. "It can really help pass the time."

Robecca wasn't the type of ghoul to hold Ramses de Nile's history with her father against Cleo; she was far too kindhearted.

"And by *hobby*, Robecca means an activity that does not involve looking in the mirror," Rochelle clarified, then pulled out a chair and sat down.

"There's no need to curtsy, Venus. Or rather there

is, since I'm royalty, but seeing as this is an informal meeting, I'm willing to bypass normal protocol," Cleo explained.

"How generous of you!" Venus quipped before engaging in an epic eye roll.

"So we all know my father seriously messed up. Like, majorly. Like, worse than the ghoul who gave me that horrible haircut last year," Cleo said, a solemn expression washing over her face. "I still can't get over it. I mean, who cuts bangs that short?"

Cleo paused, pursed her lips, and then gently ran her fingers through her hair.

"And even though Father promised to make things right, he's yet to return. So I decided to clean out his tomb and turn it into an extra closet. But Father has even more clothes than I do, so it took me a while to watch the staff lug all those gauze suits out of there."

"Is this why you called us here at eight thirty in the

morning, to discuss your new closet? Come on, ghouls, if we leave now, we can still make breakfast in the Creepateria," Venus instructed Robecca and Rochelle.

"Not so fast," Cleo snapped.

"If you expect us to curtsy, I'm afraid it's not going to happen," Rochelle explained, shaking her head.

"I didn't call you here to talk about my closet plans; I called you here to show you what I *found* hidden inside his tomb," Cleo continued.

The gold-skinned diva then pulled a mechanical box from her bag. After a few seconds of prodding, a photograph and a crisp blue envelope were revealed beneath one of the panels.

"Of all the terrible things my father has done, this is by far the worst. I'm really sorry, Robecca," Cleo said, her eyes misting. "My father hid Hexiciah away for all these years, terrified that if he ever got out, he would reveal the truth. . . ."

"And here I thought he had gotten lost while exploring the catacombs," Robecca murmured almost inaudibly.

Venus and Rochelle gently took the blue envelope from Robecca as she continued to gaze at the photo of her father.

"It's some kind of map," Venus whispered to Rochelle.

"While my cartography skills are a little rusty, it's clear that it's meant to lead us to Hexiciah Steam. And from the looks of it, he appears to be somewhere in the Little Crop of Horrors region," Rochelle assessed quickly.

"Father used to take Nefera and me to the Little Crop of Horrors for holidays when we were kids. It was a major tourist destination for monsters like my dad who missed the Old World. And to be honest, it was actually pretty claw-some," Cleo remembered before looking up at the trio of ghouls and adding sincerely, "Good luck finding Hexiciah in the Little Crop of Horrors. I know that if anyone can do it, you ghouls can."

The Little Crop of Horrors had historically been a farming region dedicated to growing such monster staples as snarling barley and thornflakes. But then, about a century earlier, small groups of monsters from the Old World started settling in the area and building towns reminiscent of the ones they had left back home. Much like an attraction at Grislyland, there were miniature versions of Transylvania, Bitealy, Scaris, etc., all conveniently located a short distance from Salem.

"Robecca, *ma chérie*? Are you okay?" Rochelle asked while Cleo exited the Study Howl, leaving the trio alone to absorb the information.

"Ramses de Nile kidnapped my father! And Cleo

just gave us a map to find him! I'm so excited and overwhelmed I'm afraid my boiler might burst! My plates might snap! My gears might grind themselves to dust!" Robecca exploded, steam pouring out of her eyes, ears, nose, and mouth.

"It is a lot to take in," Venus remarked, and then began waving her hand in an attempt to circulate the clouds of steam. "Wow, it's getting kind of hard to breathe in here."

"Never mind breathing, we have a father to find!" Rochelle announced excitedly, and then paused. "I was not being serious; one must always breathe, unless of course you are a ghost. Now then, we need to go to Little Fanghai, followed by Little Transylvania, which is a lot of ground to cover. So the sooner we leave the better."

According to the map, which included handwritten notes next to each stop, the journey to find Hexiciah Steam was to begin in the hamlet of Little Fanghai. Once there, they were to extract a golden tooth from a bearded dragon known only as Long Tail. Then, with tooth in hand, the ghouls were to head to the next town over, Little Transylvania, and present it to the infamous Count Gorelock, aka Hexiciah Steam's gatekeeper.

"Egad! I am barely able to control my excitement," Robecca yelped while standing on the train platform surrounded by Rochelle, Venus, Miss Sue Nami, and Headmistress Bloodgood.

"Remember, non-adult entities, sleeping on trains leads to missed destinations, so stay awake." Miss Sue Nami grunted and then patted each ghoul encouragingly on the arm.

"I do wish you would let us come with you," Headmistress Bloodgood added.

"*Merci boo-coup*, Madame, but I think we're more likely to blend in without you," Rochelle replied.

"Well, you know where to find us if you need us," Headmistress Bloodgood offered. "Oh! I almost forgot! Frankie Stein wanted me to give this to you."

"Her lucky plaid locket with silver stitching? That's so sweet!" Robecca gushed, and then stashed the small trinket in her front pocket.

After quickly hugging Headmistress Bloodgood and waving at Miss Sue Nami, the trio turned and boarded the train.

"I do not wish to be impolite, for I understand your extreme excitement. But for the sake of our fellow passengers, try to control your steam," Rochelle cautioned Robecca.

"Jeepers! I don't know if I can! I'm about to see my father for the first time in a century!"

"You can always stick your head out the window

if someone complains," Venus suggested with a smirk as they took their seats.

Less than an hour had passed when the train pulled into Little Fanghai. Filled with red pagodas and clusters of wild bamboo and lily ponds, it was a most peaceful and quiet village. Why, upon entering, Venus, Rochelle, and Robecca were struck by the ghostly silence.

"Are we sure this place isn't abandoned?" Venus asked as she peered around, desperate for either sight or sound of a local.

"We do not know how long ago Ramses created the map, so there is a possibility that it's *désuet*, or outdated, as you say," Rochelle answered.

"I knew I shouldn't have gotten my hopes up so soon. Like my father always said, don't count your bolts until they're tightened," Robecca droned, clearly overcome with disappointment.

"*Chérie,*" Rochelle began, and then paused, having spotted something in the distance. "*Regardez!* There's a woman!"

By the time the gold-skinned, gray-haired dragon was within earshot of the trio, they were all but jumping out of their skin to speak to her.

"Hey there, hi, hello?" Venus called out.

"*Boo-jour,* Madame, we are sorry to disturb you, but might we ask you a question?"

The elderly creature looked straight into Rochelle's eyes and nodded.

"Are you familiar with a dragon known as Long Tail?" Venus interjected excitedly.

Again the woman nodded.

"*Fangtastique!* Now, if you would be so kind as to point us in his direction," Rochelle responded.

"No."

"No? As in 'no, you would not be so kind as to point

us in his direction'?" Venus repeated incredulously.

"Yes, that is correct," she answered, and then continued on her way.

"I'm definitely starting to see why Little Fanghai isn't much of a tourist destination for Boo World folk," Venus remarked wryly.

"Broken bolts! What are we going to do?" Robecca blathered with steam billowing out of her nostrils.

"*Ne t'inquiètes pas*! There aren't that many houses. We'll just have to go door to door," Rochelle responded, and then started toward the row of identical red pagodas. "*Boo-la-la*, the poor mailman, every house looks exactly the same."

The ghouls had come to their fourth door when Robecca spotted a dragon with a tail twice the length of his body walking up to the pagoda next to them.

"His name is Long Tail, right?" Robecca double-checked with the others.

"Yeah, why?" Venus replied.

"*Et voilà*," Rochelle answered. "That must be him; I've never seen a tail of such length in my life. It's liable to get caught in something. If I were him, I would wrap it around my neck like a scarf. Or at the very least hang a sign at the end."

"Any ideas for how to approach him?" Venus asked, and then started for the door.

"Paragraph 12.3 of the Gargoyle Code of Ethics clearly states that honesty is always the best policy."

"I'm with the Gargoyle Code of Ethics! Let's just tell him the truth: that we need to yank one of his teeth out so we can find my father. . . . Actually, hearing what that sounds like, maybe we should explore other options. . . ." Robecca trailed off.

"Perhaps we do not need to tell him anything at

all," Rochelle pondered while peering through the dragon's window. "He just fell asleep while chewing his sandwich, which leads me to believe that he might be narcoleptic."

And so, a few minutes later, the ghouls found themselves pulling open the old dragon's cavernous mouth in search of a gold tooth.

"He must floss with razor blades; I've never seen such sharp teeth. If this guy wakes up, we're ghosts," Venus muttered.

"Ghosts? I cannot say that I concur with that assessment. However, missing a limb? Most definitely," Rochelle countered.

"If only we had invited Wydowna Spider. With six arms, it wouldn't matter so much if she lost one," Robecca said as she shook her head. "And I don't even see a gold filling, never mind an entire gold tooth."

"That's because it's not in his mouth," Venus

announced, and then removed a gold tooth from a chain draped around the dragon's neck.

"Who are you? And what do you think you are doing?" Long Tail growled upon suddenly snapping awake.

"Who? Us? We're nothing more than a figment of your imagination. A boring, forgettable part of your dream. Now go back to sleep, shhhhh. . . ." Robecca offered as she, Venus, and Rochelle quietly stepped away from the dragon and he once again nodded off.

"That was pretty easy," Venus delighted prematurely, still unaware of what awaited them in Little Transylvania—the infamous, the miserable, the ruthless Count Gorelock.

"*We're off to see my father, the most wonderful father of all!*" Robecca sang while literally skipping out of the town of Little Fanghai with her friends close behind.

Little Transylvania was located less than an hour's walk down a bamboo-lined path from Little Fanghai. However, as the trio approached the new town, the trees slowly began to change from bamboo to pine. And the weather grew hotter with each step they took. These were just two of the many differences they saw as they entered Little Transylvania—a quaint hamlet complete with cobblestone streets, gothic towers, oil-burning lamps, and throngs of velvet-clad vampires with well-polished fangs and exceptionally pale skin.

"Velcome to Little Transylvania! May ve offer you some Never Fail, Always Pale sunscreen?" an elderly vampire greeted the ghouls as they walked down the main street of Little Transylvania.

"Gee whiz, that's awfully nice of you. Not that I need sunscreen as I'm crafted out of copper, but my plant friend here may," Robecca responded cheerfully.

"Then let this be my gift to you," the woman said as she pressed a bottle into Venus's hand before she could say anything.

"Madame, you really are too kind," Rochelle interjected. "I was, in fact, just starting to worry that my ghoulfriend might wilt in the afternoon sun."

"Vould you like some food?" the woman asked, and then waved a young boy and ghoul over from across the street.

Venus couldn't help but smile as the two approached, dressed in identical black velvet shorts and suspenders.

"Vhat beautiful skin you have," the young ghoul squealed upon seeing Venus's bright green complexion.

"Thanks," Venus replied before turning to her friends. "This just might be the warmest welcome I've ever received."

"Children, run off and bring our lovely guests some ghoulash," the old woman instructed.

"Busting bolts, that sure is kind of you, and heaven knows we are hungry, but after more than a century without seeing my father, I just don't think I can wait any longer!" exclaimed Robecca.

"*Mais bien sûr*, but of course! That is only natural," Rochelle responded to her friend, and then looked to the old woman. "We've come to see Count Gorelock—"

However, before Rochelle could even finish her sentence, she was interrupted by the sound of wailing from the small children. With tears streaming down their now blotchy faces, Rochelle paused, unsure what to make of the situation.

"Not him! Not him!" the young boy cried, before grabbing his sister's hand, sprinting across the street, and disappearing down a small alleyway.

"Vhy vould you vant to see *him*?" the old woman inquired suspiciously.

"He has my father."

"Your poor, poor father," the old woman replied, shaking her head.

"Uh-oh," Venus groaned.

"He is an evil man. . . ."

"*Evil* is a strong word. Are you sure you don't mean grumpy or moody?" Venus pressed the woman.

"He is the reason we do not have visitors—"

"Count Gorelock?" Robecca interrupted.

"Do not say his name! We do not say his name! He is awful! He takes our food! He takes our pets! He takes everything! He is nothing but a miserable thief!"

"The man whose name shall not be spoken sounds absolutely dreadful, worse than a dry boiler. But having said that, I don't suppose you could tell us where we could find him?" Robecca continued.

The old woman stared Robecca, Rochelle, and Venus in the eyes and shook her head, silently condemning their decision. However, sensing that the trio would not be derailed from their mission, she pointed to a dilapidated castle on the hill.

Crumbling limestone, rusted rot iron, and overgrown weeds greeted the ghouls after they weathered the nearly one thousand steps needed to reach the top.

"Evil is a pretty harsh description," Robecca said nervously.

"You know old ladies; they love to exaggerate," Venus tried to reassure her friend, albeit unconvincingly.

"Do you hear singing?" Rochelle asked the others before creeping around the corner of the gothic-style building.

"Singing? How evil could Count Gorelock be if there's singing in his house?" Venus wondered.

"Deary me! That hair! Those faces!" Robecca

whispered to her friends as she looked into the castle's kitchen, where four of the gangliest ogres she had ever seen slaved over bubbling vats.

"*Quelle horreur!* Their hygiene actually appears to be worse than the trolls' at school. And that is saying something," Rochelle grumbled.

It was a memory that still stung: the granite-bodied ghoul's inability to teach the trolls of Monster High about such modern wonders as shamboo, conditioner, and antiboocterial soap.

"Well, at least they look happy. Who knows? Maybe Count Gorelock isn't so bad after all?" Robecca hoped aloud as the trio crept past the kitchen windows and up a set of stairs into the first of many dust-and-mold-ridden rooms.

"Jeepers! What are these little flies doing? They're jamming up my gears!" Robecca yelped, breathing in the thick and musty air.

"That's better than what they're doing to me; they're biting me!" Venus moaned.

"They're vampire gnats," Rochelle stated authoritatively to the others. "They are ruthless insects, not to mention greedy. They will literally eat themselves to death."

"Their teeth feel like glass shards ripping into my arm," Venus whimpered.

"They're really messing with my joints!" Robecca added.

"I may have a solution for these little parafrights. Follow me," Rochelle instructed the others, and then flung her arms around in a feeble attempt to ward off the insects.

"You can't be serious," Robecca said with a gasp upon realizing what Rochelle had in mind. "Medieval armor?"

"Do you have a better idea?" Venus quipped.

"No, I don't," Robecca acquiesced.

And so Robecca, Rochelle, and Venus each slipped on a metal suit, which not only kept the gnats at bay, but made more noise than any of them knew possible. Why, even the smallest movements resulted in a boisterous mélange of metal clanking.

"I think it's safe to assume that Count Gorelock knows we're here," Venus proclaimed, banging her way down the warped wood-paneled hall.

"I am in complete agreement, but really, what choice did we have?" Rochelle said upon opening the door to a dark and stale library.

"This place could use some potpourri," Robecca added. "Not to mention a steam cleaning."

"I'll be sure to keep that in mind." A gravelly voice cut through the room as a burgundy leather chair spun around.

Seated in the grand winged-back chair was the surprisingly petite Count Gorelock. With beady black eyes, saggy skin, and a scaly bald head, it was hard to describe the vampire as anything other than weathered.

"*Nous sommes désolées*, that is, we are very sorry to simply drop in on you unannounced," Rochelle apologized.

"But you see we have something for you," Venus chimed in.

"Pus pastries? Ghoulash? I have enough of those to last a lifetime," Count Gorelock grunted.

"No, to be honest, none of us really excel at Home Ick," Robecca admitted before placing the gold tooth on Count Gorelock's desk.

His long, spindly fingers reached for the shiny object with such speed that the ghouls fretted he might eat it, especially after he popped it into his mouth. But alas, the man was only biting it to check that it was in fact real gold.

"What is this?" he grunted, baring his gray fangs.

"What do you mean, what is this? It's what Ramses de Nile instructed us to bring so that Hexiciah Steam may be released," Venus replied strongly.

"Who are these Ramses and Hexiciah you speak of? Are they the new ogres in the kitchen?"

"Grinding gears, I knew this was too good to be true," Robecca blustered, steam gushing out of her ears and nostrils at an alarming rate.

The combination of steam and armor made for a very uncomfortable situation. So uncomfortable in fact that the copper-plated ghoul grabbed hold of her metal headpiece and yanked it off.

"It's you . . ." Count Gorelock uttered quietly, his face awash in disbelief.

"Excuse me?" Robecca replied as she fanned herself in an attempt to cool down.

"I would recognize you anywhere. After all, I've seen your picture every day for over a century."

"Hexiciah is here, isn't he?" Rochelle asked, prompting Count Gorelock to stand and pull a lever on the wall, exposing a round vault-like door.

"At first I kept Hexiciah here because Ramses was paying me, but then we became friends and it no longer felt right," Count Gorelock confessed while fiddling with the vault door. "Real friends aren't easy to come by. Not for me, anyway."

"Yeah, we did get the feeling that you weren't the most popular guy in Little Transylvania," Venus answered candidly.

"So I let Hexiciah go. And though I myself wanted to leave many times, I couldn't. He had entrusted me with something far too precious to simply leave it behind," Count Gorelock explained.

Just then, the vault door opened to reveal a sunny laboratory with vials of liquid, Bunsen burners, and a large portrait of Robecca Steam mounted on the wall.

"He's not here," Robecca mumbled with palpable disappointment as she looked into the dust-filled laboratory.

"Your father always believed that one day you would come looking for him," Count Gorelock said upon handing her an old metal tool kit with a handcrafted name tag that read MISS ROBECCA STEAM, "which is why he left this in my care to give to you."

Robecca took hold of the box as Rochelle and Venus threw their arms around her and whispered into her ears.

"One day soon, you'll find him. I just know it," Venus offered reassuringly.

The journey back to Monster High was chock-full of emotion, for Robecca had to come to terms with the fact that she still didn't know her father's whereabouts.

"I know you're sad and frustrated, but aren't you even the tiniest bit curious to see what your father left for you?" Venus questioned a glum-faced Robecca.

"I really thought he was going to be there, right up until Count Gorelock opened the door to the empty laboratory," Robecca lamented while fiddling with the tool kit's metal handle.

"Hexiciah may not have been there, but he left that box for you. Don't you think you should at least see what's inside?" Rochelle questioned Robecca, prompting the copper ghoul to slowly open the metal box.

"Tools? Well, I guess that makes sense, seeing as it's a tool box," Venus observed.

"Not just tools," Robecca said, pulling a yellowing piece of paper out from beneath a spindly-looking screwdriver.

My dearest daughter,
While time is what keeps us apart,
it is also what will eventually
bring us back together. But until
then, here are the tools you need
to properly understand it.
                              Father

"Holy bolts and screws! It's the tools to fix my internal clock!" Robecca squealed. "Do you know what this means?"

"We might actually be able to sleep through the night now?" Venus said with a laugh.

"You'll be on time for class!" Rochelle squealed. "What a relief! I've always found your tardiness quite worrisome."

While it wasn't how Robecca had planned to return to Monster High, the tool kit had managed to buoy her spirits. After all, a functioning internal clock had been atop her wish list ever since she was reassembled.

Upon returning to Monster High's purple-checkered corridors, the trio quickly noted a change in their peers. Everyone was walking in a most unusual manner—their arms stretched out in front of them, lurching backward and forward.

"Jeepers, ghoulfriends!! Do you know what this is?" Robecca screeched with excitement. "A flash mob! To welcome us home!"

"Monster High rules," Venus remarked as she shook her head, absolutely dumbfounded by the thoughtfulness of their classmates.

"*Regardez!* Frankie! Slo Mo! Draculaura! Why, even Cleo's gotten in on it!" Rochelle noted while the monsters staggered past them like zombies.

Robecca, Rochelle, and Venus couldn't resist joining in the fun and dancing around like zombies. However, the long day soon caught up with them, sending the trio straight to their beds.

Robecca, Rochelle, and Venus slept soundly, overwhelmed by the kindness of their friends. And while it turned out that the so-called flash mob was actually the result of one of Ghoulia Yelps's science projects gone awry, no one ever had the heart to tell them. Everyone, even Cleo, agreed that after all that Robecca, Rochelle, and Venus had done for Monster High, they deserved a celebration.

"Hey, ghoulfriends," Cleo called out while approaching Robecca, Rochelle, and Venus the following morning in the Creepateria. "How claw-some was my zombie walk yesterday?"

"Killer!" Venus responded honestly as Cleo started to walk away before pausing and turning toward Robecca.

"I'm really sorry you didn't find Hexiciah. I know how hard it is to be without your father. Although, not for much longer—I just heard that my father is returning to Salem. And you know what that means? He's going to want his tomb back!

Ugh!" Cleo griped and then strutted away.

"You know, I may not have found my father, but I definitely found my family," Robecca said with a smile before pulling Rochelle and Venus in for a hug.

"Ghoulfriends forever!"

An excerpt from

The Gargoyle Code of Ethics

An Introduction by Rochelle Goyle

It is often said that life, or unlife, as the case may be, does not come with a manual. However, that simply is not true, at least where gargoyles are concerned.

We stone-bodied creatures have an extensive collection of advice and guidance, which we use to govern ourselves, known as the Gargoyle Code of Ethics. And though memorizing a 1,714-page book might sound boring to other creatures, we absolutely adore it! But then again, rule making is one of Scaris's national pastimes. Enjoy some of my favorite entries from my culture's most cherished work, the Gargoyle Code of Ethics.

Paragraph 1.7

One must warn others of danger. If there is an imminent danger to a fellow entity, the one possessing such knowledge must uphold his or her duty to inform such entity so as to prevent harm befalling said entity—i.e., someone in danger.

Paragraph 3.5

Do not ask others to do for you what you can do for yourself.

Paragraph 3.9

One must share with the authorities any and all information relating to a possible crime.

Paragraph 4.7

One must not wait to help another. Help must be given right away—vite!

Paragraph 5.8

An ethical gargoyle must inform others of misconceptions. This protects them from misunderstanding and then misrepresenting themselves and/or others.

Paragraph 5.9

If one hears inaccurate information being shared, it is advised to intercept and correct the information.

Paragraph 6.8

A gargoyle must abide by his or her word. Truth must be held in the highest esteem, above all other things.

Paragraph 6.9

Being forthright in times of crisis is paramount to escaping said times. Do not waste time with pleasantries when the stakes are high.

Paragraph 7.9

Once a gargoyle has decided to help, actions should be both focused and speedy.

Paragraph 10.4

One is strongly encouraged to carry *un mouchoir*, a handkerchief. It will indubitably come in handy.

Paragraph 11.3

One must never allow poor timing to interfere with the truth. (See paragraph 6.8.)

Paragraph 11.5

It is advised that gargoyles should never sit atop normal furniture, or pets. Keep an eye out for things of delicacy and do not crush them.

Paragraph 12.3

True friendship requires honesty.

Paragraph 13.3

When in the company of candles, long-haired ghouls must pull back their hair to avoid follicular fires.

Paragraph 14.8

When taking a photo with a flash, it is imperative that the photographer keep his or her hand perfectly still. This is advised when taking any photograph.

Paragraph 18.4

One mustn't pressure others to do things they are not ready to do. Offer your guidance, advise what the Gargoyle Code of Ethics would suggest in the situation, and step back so they can make their own choice.

Paragraph 47.6

It is most important to get plenty of rest. Fatigue is a well-known reason for underachievement.

Paragraph 56.3

Do not be late for class. Any class. Don't be late for any appointment. Punctuality is preferred in all cases. Other monsters will feel slighted, and it is the height of rudeness to be late.

Paragraph 56.8

When a student is taking a class, it is important to respect monsters in authority, meaning the teachers. Students should not fib to teachers and should always tell the truth. (See paragraph 6.8.) Do not interrupt during lectures, and always take detailed notes. Do not ever interrupt any safety lessons; in fact, it is advised to memorize every word for later recall.

Paragraph 58.5

It is imprudent to have livestock or horses in the same room as food.

Paragraph 61.2

The customer is always right in business transactions, except when they are wrong or have inaccurate information. In that case, it is one's duty to correct the customer and clear up any misconceptions.

Paragraph 65.9

One should not jump to conclusions based on circumstantial evidence. Do not make assumptions on hearsay.

Paragraph 76.2

Managing a friend's expectations is key to maintaining a lifelong friendship. If you are always late, make sure they always expect you to be late.

Paragraph 76.7

Do not mix romance and friendship. Do not mess with another monster's monster.

Paragraph 77.3

It is best to not ask for favors. However, it can sometimes be necessary in order to follow another ethical practice, or in times of crisis. If you do need a favor, clearly state what you need and why you are asking. Offer to do a kindness in exchange.

Paragraph 80.7

Mission leaders must have a plan before beginning the task. A poor plan is worse than no plan at all.

Paragraph 100.1

Brush your teeth or fangs regularly. It's also important to floss daily.

Paragraph 100.7

It's always appropriate to be well and neatly dressed. It is acceptable to tailor your ensemble for the occasion.

Paragraph 100.8

One must wear appropriate clothing for secret outings. Generally, secret outings happen at night or in darkness, and therefore black is recommended.

Paragraph 125.7

If one has concerns or misgivings, or suspects judgments or actions may be based on misconceptions or half-truths, it's always better to voice such concerns sooner rather than later.

Paragraph 200.1

The code and its rules may be broken ONLY when the results of said action will aid in the greater good—for example, if it will save a monster's life.